Up, Up and Away

Written by Monica Hughes

The bubbles go up,
up, up and away.

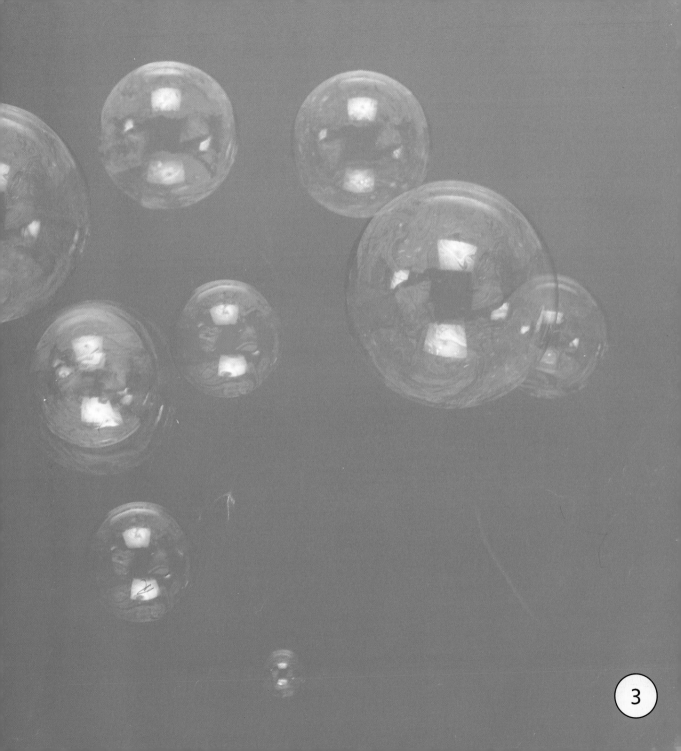

The fireworks go up,
up, up and away.

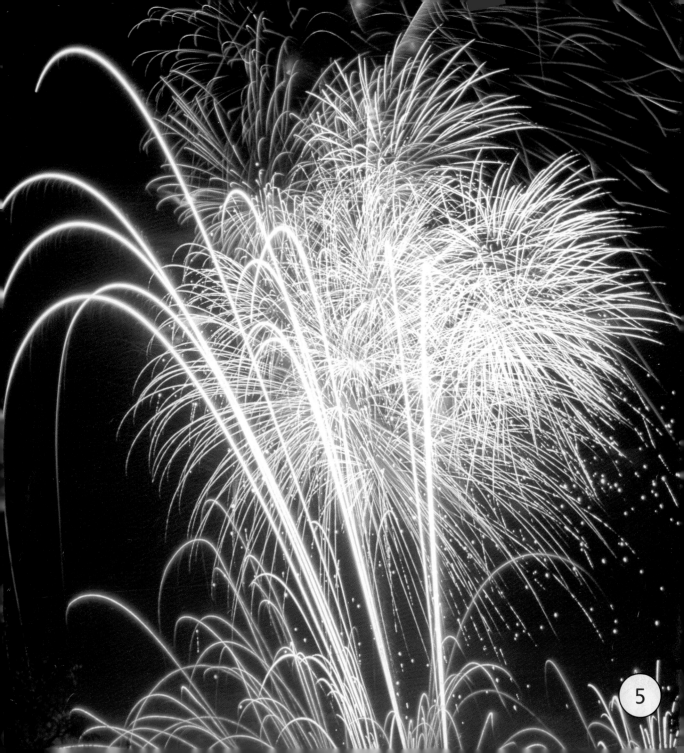

The balloons go up,
up, up and away.

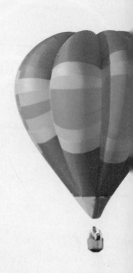

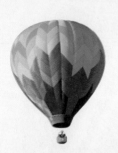

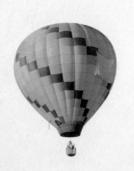

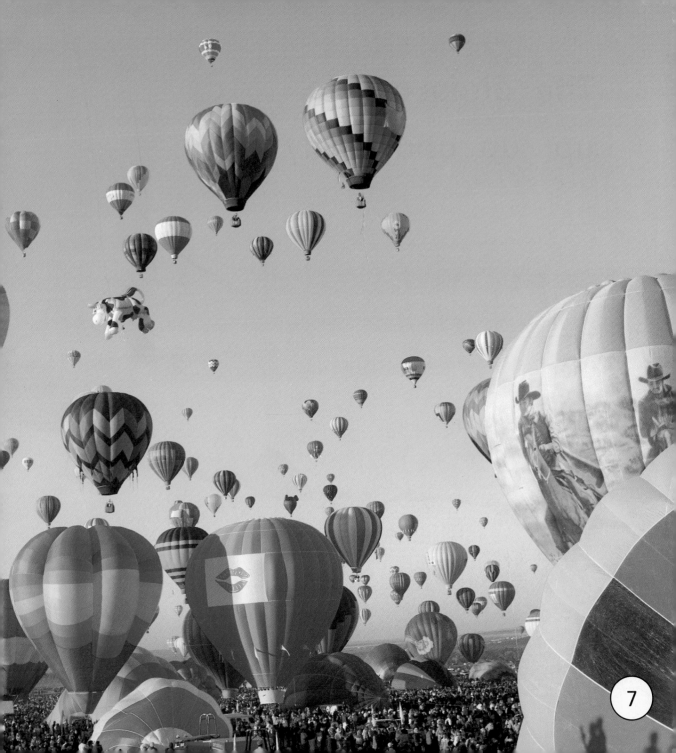

The birds go up,
up, up and away.

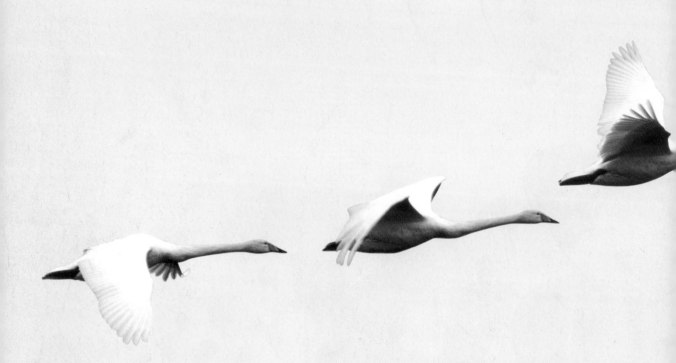

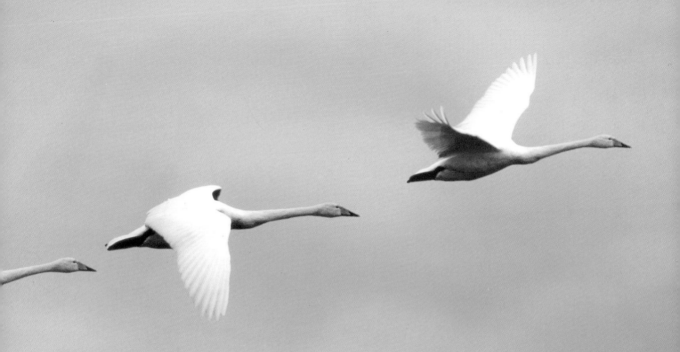

The planes go up...

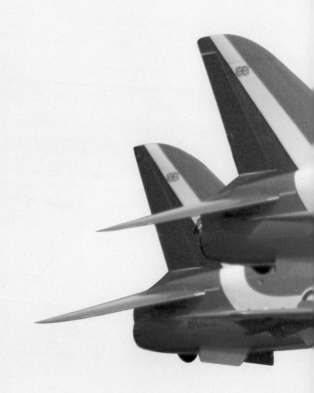

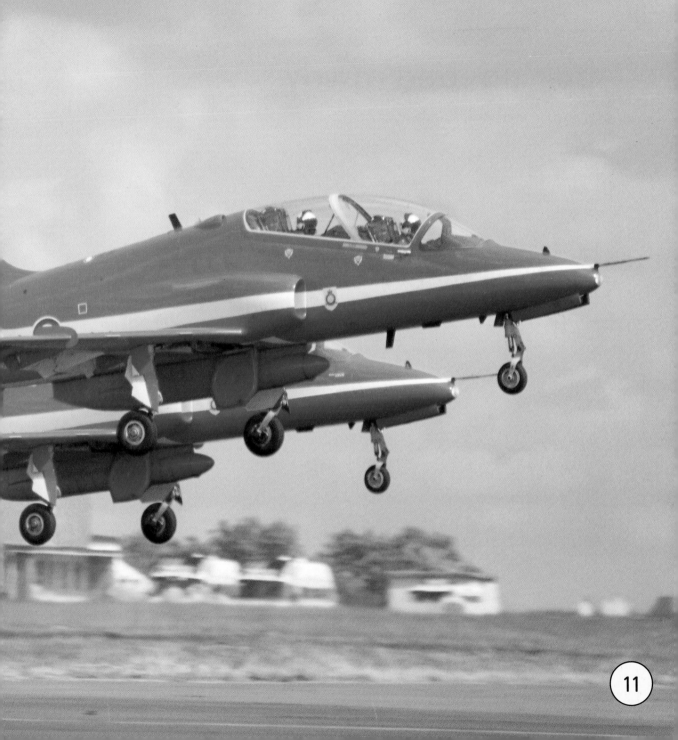

up, up and away.